DreamWorks

Trolls

Look and Find®

Princess Poppy looks forward to the happy day when she will be the Queen of all Troll Village! In the meantime, she's busy keeping her scrapbooks up to date.

Find these mementos in Poppy's book:

- color wheel
- rainbow patch
- baby picture
- wrapper from a favorite cupcake
- hug sticker
- sheet music

TRUE COLORS
TIME for a HUG

All Trolls agree that there's more to life than cupcakes and rainbows. For most, there's glitter too! But for Branch, life is a bit more...worrisome. He's always on the lookout for Troll-eating Bergens.

Can you find these emergency supplies in Branch's survival bunker?

life preserver

Bergen repellent

candle

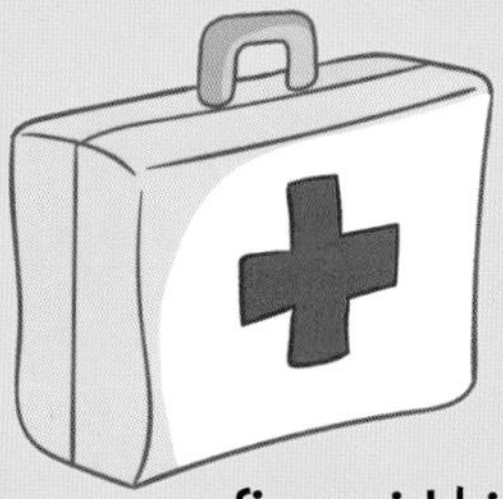

first-aid kit

cupcakes

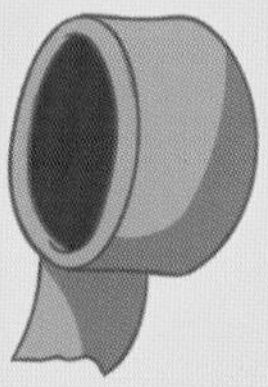

duct tape

EMERGENCY
CUPCAKES

Want a cupcake? Biggie always does! He's looking for his favorite flavors on the cupcakery's shelves.

Can you help Biggie find these tasty treats?

DJ Suki is holding auditions for her next critter-inspired music track. She can find the beat in every Skitterboard and the crescendo in every Caterbus!

Can you find these up-and-coming music makers?

this Glowfly

this Caterbus

this Humworm

this Chorusfly

this Glowfly

this Sparkbug

King Gristle of Bergen Town would love a slice of Troll pizza. Luckily, it's not on the menu...yet. Gristle will have to be happy with the current selection.

Look around for these peculiar pies:

pickle pizza

hot dog pizza

ice cream pizza

lollipop pizza

fruit pizza

veggie pizza

Satin and Chenille may be twins, but they never wear the same outfit at the same time. They're much too creative for lookalike styles!

Can you spot these clothing choices in the closet chaos?

- this sock
- this belt
- jumpsuit
- these earrings
- this dress
- this scarf

After twenty years of searching, Chef has finally found the Trolls! She is determined to take them back to Bergen Town...as the centerpiece of her Trollstice dinner menu.

These Trolls are trying to hide from Chef. Can you find them... before she does?
Smidge
Cooper
this Troll child
Fuzzbert
Biggie
King Peppy

Poppy and her pals are ready to celebrate what makes each Troll special. The best time to show off your true colors is always...now!

Can you find these colorful components at Poppy's party?

- a pink hair bow
- this orange hair
- this green hat
- a yellow jewel
- these purple pants
- a blue flower

Princess Poppy's coronation daydreams find their way into her scrapbooks too. Turn back to her tome to find these sovereign scribbles:

Branch hasn't found his true colors yet. But there *are* colors waiting to be found—even in his bunker! Bop back to the bunker to find something that is:

Bustle back to Biggie to spot these cupcakery contraptions:

DJ Suki's audition has attracted a sextet of swinging Skitterboards! Shoot back to the show and find these multi-colored Skitterboard musicians:

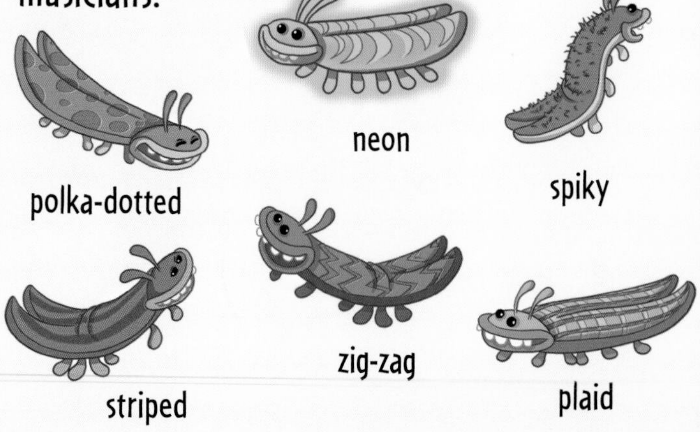

Once upon a time, the kitchens of Bergen Town were famous for their Troll recipes. No more! Pop back to the banquet hall to spot these foods whose names start with **t**, like **T**roll.

Satin and Chenille are a perfect pair of BFFFs—Best Fashion Friends Forever! Wander back to their wardrobe to find more pretty pairs each friend can wear:

Everything in Troll Village is trying to hide from Chef! Circle back to the catastrophe to spot these concerned creatures:

Who's the star of the party? Guy Diamond! He leaves a little sparkle wherever he goes.

Look back through the book to find one of Guy's sparkly smidgens in the party scene and in every other picture.